LEAP

WRITTEN BY CAMPBELL MANNING

ILLUSTRATED BY NADIA RONQUILLO

Designed by Flowerpot Press
in Franklin, TN.
www.FlowerpotPress.com
Designer: Stephanie Meyers
Editor: Katrine Crow
ROR-0811-0113
ISBN: 978-1-4867-1267-0
Made in China/Fabriqué en Chine

OH!

Just one last thing:
I have a hunch
Mom makes me wait
'til after lunch.

And then they'll cheer
and scream and cry,
"Did you just see
that HERO FLY?!?"

The crowd won't make
a single sound
as I float down
and touch the ground.

Sailing swiftly,
    through sun and clouds,
I will AMAZE
    the giant crowds!

And after I
    have flown and soared,
I'll just lie back
    and PULL THE CORD!

Then falling down
    through outer space,
I'll have a grin
    upon my face.

And when I reach
    the atmosphere,
I'll know the time
    is almost here.

These memories
are mine to keep.
I'll lock them in
and then I'll

LEAP!

I'll see the Earth from way up high
and satellites as they pass by.

Stars shining brighter than before,
up where the universe can roar!

And I'm not one
        to brag or gloat,
but when I reach
        the moon, I'll float!

Now I'm all set.
    My ship's all packed.
The tank is full.
    Supplies are stacked.

And so that I can breathe up there,
I'll bring a zillion cans of air.

I'll bring some spaceman snacks as well.
I will get hungry. I can tell.

I hear it's cold, but here's the thing,
  I have long underwear to bring.

And I will need a warm coat, too.
  My furry, fluffy one might do.

I'll need to get
    outer space stuff.
I hope that I
    can find enough.

Not any ship
    will do the trick.
It must be big
    and really quick.

A normal plane
    can't make the trip.
I'll have to build
    a rocket ship!

And I'm not scared,
no, not one bit.
I'll prove it soon
—I'm doin' it!

But I'll show them.
I know I can!
Soon they'll all see
that I'M THE MAN!

Nobody thinks
my plan will work.
They think my brain
has gone BERSERK!

My friends all laugh.
    They call me nuts.
They say that I
    don't have the guts.

I thought I'd jump
   off of a star.
For my first time,
   that seemed too far.

Maybe not now,
  but pretty soon,
I'm going to LEAP
  off of the moon!